THE LITTLE MERMAID

WALT DISNEY'S CLASSIC

THE LITTLE
MERMAID

Based on Disney's
full-length animated movie

Adapted by Jan Carr

SCHOLASTIC INC.
New York Toronto London Auckland Sydney

ISBN 0-590-42988-4

© 1989 The Walt Disney Company. All rights reserved.
Published by Scholastic Inc.

12 11 10 9 8 7 6 5 4 3 2   9/8 0 1 2 3 4/9

Printed in the U.S.A.   28

First Scholastic printing, November 1989

THE LITTLE MERMAID

1

Not everyone believes in mermaids. A lot of landlubbers think the very idea is fishy. But those who spend time at sea know better. They know that the ocean is deep and that it holds many secrets. Down below the waves live other creatures — creatures who know as little about us as we do about them. It is not often that the two worlds meet.

This story starts out at sea, with sailors on a ship. The day was blustery, and the ocean was choppy. Rough waves tossed the ship to and fro. The sailors rushed about the deck, battening down hatches and tightening rigging. As they worked, they sang a sea chantey. The words told of a kingdom at the bottom of the sea. A merkingdom, they called it. A kingdom with mermaids and mermen, too.

The sailors sang their song for a special passenger, Prince Eric. It was the Prince's eighteenth birthday. Prince Eric rushed about the deck, helping the sailors any way he could.

"Isn't this great?" he said. "The salty sea air! The wind at your face! A perfect day to be at sea!"

"Aye, that it is, lad," smiled the sailor working beside him.

Eric's dog Max jumped up to help, too. Max was a big, woolly sheepdog. He loved the sea as much as his master did.

Across the deck, though, there was someone who did not look so happy. This was Sir Grimsby, Eric's guardian. Sir Grimsby was feeling seasick. He leaned against the ship's rail. His face was pale, and he clutched his stomach woozily.

One of the sailors took a big, hearty breath.

"A fine, strong wind and a following sea," he said. "King Triton must be in a friendly-type mood."

Eric looked up from his work.

"King Triton?" he asked.

"Why, ruler of the merpeople, lad," another sailor joined in. "Thought every good sailor knew all about *him*."

"Merpeople!" laughed Sir Grimsby, raising his head. "Eric, pay no attention to this nautical nonsense."

"But it ain't nonsense!" shouted one of the sailors. "It's the truth! There's a whole *world* of merpeople under the sea!"

"King Triton is their ruler," said another. "He's got seven fair daughters."

"And a witch of a sister named Ursula."

"Ursula?" asked Eric.

"Evil and ugly and hungry for power," the sailors explained. "King Triton banished her off into exile. And there she lives now, just biding her time."

Prince Eric and Sir Grimsby listened carefully while the sailors explained. They said that this evil witch Ursula was still scheming and plotting to overthrow King Triton. She wanted to be Queen of the Sea.

Sir Grimsby backed up and slipped on the wet deck. He knocked against a barrel of fish. Splash! One little fish wriggled free and flung itself overboard, escaping back to its briny home.

2

The humans weren't the only ones celebrating that day. That day was also a special day in the kingdom of the merpeople. Below the hull of the ship, deep down at the bottom of the ocean, merpeople were streaming into a grand concert hall and taking their seats. The crowd watched the stage expectantly. They hushed as a little seahorse swam out onto the stage and blew his trumpet.

"His Royal Highness, King Triton!" the seahorse announced.

King Triton swam out onto the stage. He was a broad-chested merman with twinkling eyes and a long, silver beard. The crowd waved and cheered. King Triton was a good king, and the merpeople loved him.

"Hmph! Oof! Out of the way, man." A small crab pushed his way past King Triton's guards. "My public awaits me," he said. This was Sebastian, the conductor for the concert. He swam out

4

next to King Triton, flashed a big smile, and took his own bow. King Triton leaned over and whispered to the crab.

"I'm looking forward to this performance, Sebastian. I know you won't let me down."

"Ho-ho, Your Majesty." Sebastian winked. "This will be the finest concert I have ever conducted. Your daughters, they will be spectacular!"

"Yes, and especially my little Ariel," said the king. The concert was to be Ariel's debut. The king was especially proud of his youngest daughter.

"Princess Ariel?" Sebastian choked. "She has the most *beautiful* voice of all." But under his breath, he muttered, "If she'd only show up for rehearsal once in a while."

"What did you say?" King Triton asked sharply.

"Ho-ho, no problem. No problem, Your Majesty," Sebastian said sheepishly. "Ariel's debut will be perfect."

With that, Sebastian slipped through the water and took his place at the conductor's stand. He raised his hands to signal the orchestra. The orchestra began playing. As the music filled the hall, a great wash of bubbles flooded the stage. Behind the bubbles were six of King Triton's seven daughters, all brightly costumed. Each was a polished performer. The sisters swam out in formation.

They began to dance and sing. King Triton beamed proudly.

"We are the daughters of Triton," they sang. "Our father named us well."

Each of the sister mermaids swam forward to introduce herself to the audience.

"Aquata," one sang.

"Andrina," sang another.

"Arista," "Attina," "Adella," "Alana. . . ."

As the sisters sang, a large clamshell rose up from the floor of the stage. The sisters gathered around the shell.

"And then there is the youngest in her musical debut," they sang, "our seventh little sister. We're presenting her to you, to sing a song Sebastian wrote. Her voice is like a bell."

The sisters all smiled and extended their hands toward the shell to present their youngest sister. The shell began to open.

"She's our little sister, Arie —" The sisters gasped. The shell was empty!

Sebastian looked frantically toward King Triton. The King was red with anger.

"Ariel!" he shouted.

The name echoed through the concert hall and out into the ocean depths.

3

Ariel did not hear her father call her name. She
was far away, in another part of the ocean.
She was playing with her friend, a plump fish
named Flounder.

The pretty young mermaid swam quickly
through the water. Her full red hair trailed in the
water behind her.

"Ariel, wait for me!" called Flounder.

"Hurry up!" Ariel called back.

Ariel swam up to a large anchor that was lodged
in the sand. Beyond the anchor was the wreck of
a large sunken ship.

"There it is," she said. "Isn't it fantastic?"

Flounder looked nervously around. He was not
so sure he would call the wreck "fantastic." The
whole place looked kind of creepy to him.

"Yeah. Sure. It's great," he said. "Now let's get
out of here!"

"I'm going inside," said Ariel. She started to
swim toward the wreck. "If you don't want to

come, you can just stay here and watch for sharks."

Flounder jumped at the word.

"Sharks!" he cried. "Help!"

"Don't be such a guppy," Ariel laughed.

"I'm no guppy," said Flounder. He swam quickly after his friend.

The two squeezed through the narrow porthole of the sunken ship. Inside the ship, the water was dark and murky. Ariel swam up to a door. It was closed. She pried it open and swam through.

"Oh, my gosh. Oh, my *gosh!*" she cried. Her eyes darted excitedly around the room. The room was filled with everyday objects from the human world, things that had been left there by the people who had once sailed the ship. "Have you ever seen anything so wonderful in your entire life?" Ariel cried.

She picked up an old, bent fork and looked at it lovingly.

"Wow, cool!" said Flounder. "But what is it?"

"I don't know," said Ariel. "But I bet Scuttle will." She stuffed it into a pouch that she carried.

Outside the room, something creaked. Flounder jumped at the sound.

"What was that?" he said quickly. "Did you hear something?"

Ariel was still sorting through her newfound treasures. She picked up an old pipe.

"Hmm," she said, "I wonder what this one is." She slipped the pipe into her pouch, too.

A dark shadow passed outside the cabin's door. Flounder's eyes opened wide in fright.

"A-Ariel," he stuttered.

"Will you relax?" Ariel said to her friend. "Nothing's going to happen."

Flounder swam to the doorway and peered out cautiously. Just as he was about to poke his head out the door, a mouth snapped open on the other side of the door frame. The mouth was huge and had sharp, jagged teeth.

"Aaah!" Flounder screamed when he realized what it was. "Shark!"

Flounder jumped back just as the shark's jaws snapped shut. Flounder and Ariel skittered through the ship and back out through the porthole. They escaped the shark by mere inches! They streaked up through the ocean to the surface.

When they had reached safety, Flounder stuck his tongue out and called back to the shark. "You big bully!" he yelled.

Ariel shook her head and laughed at her friend.

"Flounder, you really are a guppy," she said.

4

A riel and Flounder floated at the surface of the water. Ariel was still clutching the pouch in which she had gathered her human treasures.

"Scuttle!" she called across the water. "Scuttle!"

At the other end of the bay, perched on a rock, was a rather rumpled-looking seagull. He was singing to himself and peering through the wrong end of a telescope.

"Whoa!" he said as he caught sight of Ariel. "Mermaid off the port bow! Ariel! How ya doin', kid?"

Ariel glided over to her friend and reached into her pouch to show him her treasures.

"Scuttle," she said excitedly, "look what we found!"

Scuttle peered into the bag.

"Human stuff, huh?" he said. "Hey, let me see."

Scuttle pulled the bent fork out and examined it closely.

"Look at this!" he said. "Wow! This is special. This is very, very unusual."

"What is it?" asked Ariel. Scuttle seemed to know so much about humans and their ways, and Ariel believed every word he said.

Scuttle held up the old fork.

"It's a dinglehopper," he said confidently. "Humans use these little babies to straighten out their hair. See," he said. He combed the tines of the fork through the soft feathers at the top of his head. "Just a little twirl and a yank there and . . ." His top feathers sprung out in tight ringlets. "You got yourself an aesthetically pleasin' configuration of hair that humans go nuts over."

"Oh, like this?" asked Ariel.

She combed the fork through her own hair.

"Hey, look at that!" said Scuttle. "If I didn't know better, I'd think I was conversing with a human being right now."

Ariel turned the fork over in her hands.

"A dinglehopper!" she said.

"What about this?" Flounder asked. He nodded toward the pipe Ariel had found.

"Now, this I haven't seen in years," Scuttle said. "This is wonderful."

Scuttle turned the pipe over carefully. He didn't really have any idea what it was.

"It's a snarfblatt," he declared. Ariel and Flounder leaned closer to listen to his explanation.

11

"Now, the snarfblatt dates back to prehysterical times when humans used to sit around and stare at each other all day. It got very boring. So they invented this snarfblatt to make fine music."

He picked up the pipe by its stem and lifted it to his beak to demonstrate.

"Allow me," he said.

Scuttle blew into the pipe. Nothing happened. He blew harder. Water spurted out of its bowl.

Ariel's face turned pale. Music! Suddenly Ariel remembered something. Something she had forgotten. Something important. "The concert!" she cried. "Oh, my gosh! My father's going to kill me!"

Flounder looked at her in alarm.

"The concert was today?" he asked.

"I'm sorry! I've got to go!" cried Ariel. "Thank you, Scuttle."

Ariel waved a quick good-bye to her friend. Then, with her pouch in tow and Flounder at her tail, Ariel dove swiftly back down into the sea.

5

As Ariel and Flounder hurried back home to the merkingdom, they did not know that they were being watched. Ursula, the evil sea witch, was sitting on a giant shell, peering into her pool of light, and watching their every move.

"Yes, hurry home, Princess," she sneered. "We wouldn't want to miss Daddy's celebration, now, would we?"

Ursula lowered her large, blubbery body off her shell and floated up, her tentacles wafting along behind her.

"Hah!" she cried bitterly. "*They* celebrate while *I* waste away to practically nothing. Look at me! Banished and exiled and practically starving! Well, I'll give that king something to celebrate soon enough.

"Flotsam! Jetsam!" she cried.

Two mean-eyed eels slithered out at her ca

"I want you two to keep an extra-close on this pretty little daughter of his," U structed. "I may be able to use her. She may be the key to Triton's undoing."

When Ariel arrived home, her father, the King, was waiting for her.

"I just don't know what we're going to do with you, young lady," he scolded.

"Daddy, I'm sorry," Ariel apologized. "I just forgot. I — "

Sebastian, the conductor, was angry at her, too.

"The entire celebration was ruined!" he shouted. "Completely destroyed. This concert was to be the pinnacle of my distinguished career! Now, thanks to you, I am the laughingstock of the entire kingdom!"

Flounder swam to his friend's side.

"But it wasn't her fault," he said. "See, first this shark chased us. And then this seagull came — "

"Seagull!" boomed King Triton. "You went up to the surface again, didn't you?"

"Nothing happened," Ariel protested weakly.

"Ariel," the King cut her off. "How many times must we go through this? You could have been seen by one of those barbarians! One of those *humans!*"

"Oh, Daddy," cried Ariel. "They're not barbarians. They're — "

"They are dangerous!" shouted the King. "Do you think I want to see my youngest daughter snared by some fisheater's hook?"

14

"I'm sixteen years old!" Ariel answered proudly. "I'm not a child anymore."

"Don't you take that tone of voice with me!" shouted her father. "As long as you live under my ocean, you'll obey my rules."

"But if you would just listen," pleaded Ariel.

"Not another word," said the King. "And I am never to hear of you going to the surface again! Is that clear?"

Ariel whirled around in frustration and swam off in a huff to her room.

"Hmph!" said Sebastian, as he watched her leave. "Teenagers! They think they know everything."

King Triton only sighed. "Do you think I was too hard on her?" he asked.

"Definitely not!" declared Sebastian. "If Ariel were my daughter, I'd keep her under tight control. None of this flitting to the surface and other such nonsense!"

"You're absolutely right," said the King. "Ariel needs someone to keep her out of trouble." The King looked at Sebastian. "And, Sebastian, you're just the crab to do it," he said.

The little crab jumped back in surprise. *Him?* Keep Ariel out of trouble? *That* was going to be a full-time job.

6

Sebastian was not at all happy about his new job, but the King had given him an order, and he knew he had to obey.

"How do I get myself into these situations?" he grumbled. "I should be writing symphonies, not tagging along after some headstrong teenager."

Sebastian spotted Ariel and Flounder swimming off in the distance. Ariel had her pouch clutched tightly in her hands. Sebastian took off to follow them.

Ariel and Flounder swam to a dark, shell-encrusted grotto. Sebastian slipped quietly through the doorway behind them. He was surprised at what he saw.

Inside the grotto were all sorts of objects from the human world—fishing ropes, a sword, a candelabra. Ariel reached into her pouch and placed her two new objects among the others.

"If only I could make Father understand," she said sadly. "I just don't think about things the way he does. I don't see how a world that makes such wonderful things could be bad."

Ariel looked around at all the things she had collected from the human world. In her heart, Ariel wanted to be human. She wanted to have legs instead of a tail. She wanted to live on land.

Clunk! Sebastian tumbled out of the mug where he had been hiding. Ariel whirled around at the sound.

"Sebastian!" she cried.

"Ariel," said Sebastian. "What *is* all this?"

"It's my collection," she said uneasily.

"Oh, I *see*," said Sebastian. "Your collection. If your father knew about this place. . . ."

"Oh, please, Sebastian," Ariel pleaded. "You won't tell him, will you? He'd never understand."

"Ariel," Sebastian sighed. "You're under a lot of pressure down here. Let me take you home."

Just then a large shadow passed over the crevice at the top of the grotto. Ariel looked up, entranced.

"What do you suppose that is?" she said.

Before Sebastian could stop her, Ariel was swimming out of the grotto and up toward the surface of the water. The shadow was cast by a large human ship that was passing above them. Ariel swam straight for it.

"Jumpin' jellyfish!" Sebastian cried. "Ariel, where are you going? Ariel, come back!"

17

7

Ariel rose to the surface. She saw the ship sitting regally among the waves. Bright-colored lights ringed the deck. Some of the sailors were setting off fireworks. Others were singing and dancing. Someone lifted up Prince Eric and tossed him high.

"Happy birthday!" everyone cried.

It was quite a celebration.

Ariel stared, enchanted. She could not keep her eyes off the handsome prince. She watched as he picked up a flute and started to play a merry tune, while Max, his sheepdog, pranced beside him. Scuttle flew down and perched next to Ariel.

"Hey there, sweetie. Quite a show, huh?" he said.

"Shh! Scuttle, they'll hear you," said Ariel. Her gaze drifted back to the Prince. "I've never seen a human this close before," she whispered. "He's very handsome, isn't he?"

Scuttle's eyes landed on Max.

"I don't know," he said. "He looks kind of hairy and slobbery to me."

"Not that one," said Ariel. "The one playing the snarfblatt."

On deck, Sir Grimsby made his way through the crowd and held up his hands to get everyone's attention.

"Silence! Silence!" he said. "It is now my honor and privilege to present our esteemed Prince Eric with a very special, very expensive, very large birthday present."

Eric blushed.

"Aw, Grimsby, you old beanpole, you shouldn't have," he said.

Two sailors carried out a large, heavy present that was draped in cloth and tied with bright ribbon. The sailors cut the ribbon. They pulled back the cloth. Underneath was a life-size marble statue of Prince Eric himself, in a serious, heroic pose.

"G-gee, Grim," Eric stuttered. "It's, uh, really something."

"Yes," smiled Sir Grimsby. "I commissioned it myself. Of course, I had hoped it would be a wedding present."

Prince Eric shifted uncomfortably.

"Come on, Grim, don't start," he said. "The right girl is out there somewhere. I just haven't found her yet."

"Well," said Sir Grimsby, "perhaps you haven't been looking hard enough."

"Believe me," said Eric. "When I find her, I'll know. Without a doubt, it'll just — BAM! — hit me like lightning!"

Strangely enough, as he spoke dark clouds began to gather in the sky, and a bright flash of lightning streaked across the heavens.

"It's a storm!" shouted a sailor. "Stand fast! Secure the rigging!"

The storm came up quickly. The sea began to roll and toss the ship about. Sir Grimsby grabbed the ship's rail for balance. Eric's birthday statue rolled over the side and into the churning waters.

CRACK! Another bolt of lightning hit the mast of the ship and set it on fire. Panic broke out on deck. Sailors were climbing over the ship's rail and jumping into the sea. Ariel watched frantically for Eric.

Suddenly a powder keg exploded. The explosion threw Eric overboard into the churning sea. Ariel dove down after him. She caught the Prince by the waist, pulled him back up to the surface of the water, and swam with him to shore.

8

When the storm cleared, Eric was lying on the edge of the shore, and Ariel and Scuttle were huddled around him. Eric's eyes were closed. He did not move.

"Is he dead?" asked Ariel.

Scuttle put his ear to Eric's foot.

"I can't make out a heartbeat," he said.

"No, look!" cried Ariel. "He's breathing!"

She leaned closer to the Prince and stroked his wet hair.

"He's so beautiful," she said as she gazed down at his face.

Ariel took the Prince's head and cradled it in her arms. She began to sing softly. The Prince did not open his eyes, but he stirred, and his lips formed a smile, as if he were having a most delicious dream.

The last of the storm clouds cleared, and the morning sun began to peek over the horizon. Ariel leaned down to kiss the sleeping prince. But just before her lips touched his, Max came running and barking down the sand. Sir Grimsby ran right behind him. Ariel dove back into the ocean. Eric opened his eyes slowly and blinked at the light.

"I . . . I think I've been hit by lightning," he said.

"What?" said Grimsby. "Good heavens!"

"A girl rescued me," Eric started to remember. "She was *singing*. She had the most beautiful voice."

"Ah, Eric," chided Grimsby. "I think you've swallowed too much seawater. Up we go!" He helped the young prince to his feet. "That's a good boy."

Eric looked back at the ocean. He wondered who that girl was and where she had gone. He didn't know that Ariel was still watching him. She had ducked behind a rock that jutted out farther down the shore. Sebastian was floating beside her and watching her worriedly.

"We're just going to forget this whole thing ever happened," Sebastian said firmly. "The Sea King will never know. You won't tell him. I won't tell him. I will stay in one piece!"

But Ariel didn't hear a word Sebastian was saying. She was still gazing after the Prince and dreamily humming her song.

Sebastian was not the only one watching Ariel. In her lair, Ursula was bent over her pool of light.

She could see Ariel crouched behind the rock. She had seen Ariel lean over and try to kiss the Prince.

"Oh no, no, no, no, *no!*" she cackled. "I can't stand it! It's too *easy!* The child is in love with a *human!* And not just any human, a prince! Her daddy'll love that!"

Ursula clapped her hands in glee and began dancing excitedly around the pool of light. She had an idea, and it was not a pretty one.

"It's like snatching kelp from a minnow!" she cried. "King Triton's headstrong, lovesick girl. The perfect bait when I go fishing for her father!"

9

That morning when Ariel got home, she closed herself into the dressing room she shared with her sisters and combed out her long, full hair. She clipped a pretty flower above her ear.

Ariel's sisters gathered outside the door. They wanted to use the dressing room, too.

Andrina pounded on the door.

"Ariel, dear," she called. "Time to come out. You've been in there all morning."

Aquata looked at Andrina.

"What is with her lately?" she asked.

The door swung open, and Ariel floated out dreamily. She bumped right into her father, who was swimming up to meet her.

"Morning, Daddy," she said. She planted a quick, light kiss on his cheek and continued on her way.

King Triton rubbed his cheek and stared after Ariel. Andrina shook her head and smiled.

"She's got it bad," she said.

"What has she got?" asked King Triton.

"Isn't it obvious?" said Aquata. "Ariel's in love."

King Triton looked stunned.

"Ariel . . . in love?" he said.

The King didn't quite know what to think. This news was unexpected. A slow smile broke across his face. His youngest daughter. In love. The King rather liked the idea.

Sebastian, though, was not so pleased. He knew exactly with whom Ariel had fallen in love.

"So far, so good," he said to himself. "I don't think the King knows, but it will not be easy keeping something like this a secret for long."

Sebastian found the young princess in an undersea garden. She was lounging on a rock, idly plucking petals off a flower.

"He loves me. He loves me not," she said. She got to the last petal. "He loves me!" she cried. "I knew it!"

"Ariel," snapped Sebastian. "Stop talking crazy!"

Ariel dropped her petals and began swimming back and forth.

"I've got to see him again," she said excitedly. "Tonight. Scuttle knows where he lives."

Sebastian watched the girl nervously.

"Ariel, please," he said. "Will you get your head out of the clouds and back in the water where it *belongs*?"

"I'll swim up to his castle," Ariel went on. "Then Flounder will splash around to get his attention, and then we'll — "

"Ariel!" Sebastian cut her off. "Down here is your home. The human world, it's a mess. Life under the sea is better than anything they've got up there."

Sebastian turned to point out the beauties of life undersea. When his back was turned, Flounder swam up and whispered something in Ariel's ear. Ariel's face brightened. She and Flounder slipped quietly away. When Sebastian turned back, the Princess was gone.

"Oh," he sighed. "Somebody's got to nail that girl's fins to the floor."

Just then a little seahorse swam up, a messenger from the palace.

"I've got an urgent message from the King," he announced.

"The Sea King?" gulped Sebastian.

"He wants to see you right away," said the messenger. "Something about Ariel."

Sebastian groaned to himself.

"He *knows*!" he said.

10

King Triton was waiting in his throne room. He was thinking about Ariel and the lovely wedding he would give for her.

"Let's see, now," he smiled to himself. "Who can the lucky merman be?"

Sebastian entered the room. He was quivering with fear.

"Sebastian," the King said slowly. "I'm concerned about Ariel. Have you noticed she's been acting very peculiar lately?"

"Peculiar?" gulped Sebastian.

"You know," said the King. "Mooning about, daydreaming, singing to herself. Sebastian," he smiled, "I know you've been keeping something from me."

"Keeping something?" Sebastian blinked.

"About Ariel," said King Triton. "That she's in love."

Sebastian fell at the King's feet.

"I tried to stop her, Sire," he blurted out. "She

wouldn't listen. I told her to stay away from humans."

The King's smile slowly melted. His face turned red. Anger began churning inside him.

"Humans!" he exploded. "What's this about humans?"

Across the kingdom, Ariel was following Flounder to the grotto.

"Flounder," she laughed. "Why can't you just tell me what this is all about?"

"You'll see," Flounder said proudly. "It's a surprise."

Ariel stopped short at the entrance to the grotto.

"Oh, Flounder!" she cried.

There before her was the marble statue of Prince Eric. Flounder had set it right in the center of all of Ariel's other human treasures.

"It looks just like him," Ariel gasped.

She danced around the statue.

"Why, Eric," she said playfully, as if the statue were Eric himself. "What's that you say? You want me to marry you? Why, this is all so sudden."

Ariel giggled. She twirled toward the doorway. There, in the entrance, was her father. His face was red with rage.

"Daddy!" Ariel cried.

King Triton did not yell. He looked his daughter in the eye.

"Is it true that you rescued a human from drowning?" he asked quietly.

"Daddy," Ariel whispered, "I had to."

The King frowned.

"Ariel, you know very well that contact between the human world and the merworld is strictly forbidden," he said.

"He would have died," Ariel tried to explain.

"One less human to worry about," the King said coldly.

Ariel could not believe her ears.

"But you don't even know him," she protested.

"Know him!" King Triton boomed. "I don't have to know him! Humans are all the same. Spineless, savage, harpooning fisheaters. They're incapable of any feeling!"

"Daddy, I love him!" Ariel cried.

"NO!" King Triton bellowed. The sound echoed off the walls of the grotto. "You can never be together! He's a human! You're a mermaid!"

"I don't care!" wailed Ariel.

King Triton raised his powerful spear, aimed it at Ariel's treasures, and fired. Electrical sparks shot through the room. The statue of Prince Eric shattered into a million pieces. Ariel collapsed on the floor.

"Go away!" she sobbed. "Just go away!"

11

Ariel lay alone, weeping among the ruins of her treasures. Flotsam and Jetsam, Ursula's evil eels, slithered into the grotto and leered. They knew this was their chance.

"Poor, sweet child," said Jetsam.

"Who are you?" Ariel asked, startled.

"Don't be scared," said Flotsam. "We represent someone who can help you."

"Someone who can make all your dreams come true," added Jetsam.

"Just imagine," said Flotsam. "You and your prince together forever."

"I don't understand," said Ariel. These eels looked slimy. She didn't trust them. And yet . . .

"Ursula has great powers," said Flotsam.

"The sea witch!" cried Ariel. So that was it! "No!" she yelled. "Get out of here! Leave me alone!"

"Suit yourself," shrugged Flotsam.

He picked up a piece of Eric's broken statue.

He tossed the shard of marble aside.

"Wait!" cried Ariel.

The eels smiled at each other. They knew they had her now.

"Yesss?" they hissed.

Outside the grotto, Sebastian and Flounder were huddled together, worrying about the Princess. The eels came swimming past. Ariel was swimming with them.

"Ariel!" Sebastian cried. "What are you doing with this riffraff?"

"I'm going to see Ursula," Ariel said curtly.

"Ariel!" Sebastian swam to keep up with her. "She's a demon! She's a monster! She's . . . "

Sebastian grabbed at Ariel's tail to stop her. Ariel whirled around angrily and pulled her tail free.

"Why don't you go tell my father?" she said. "You're good at that, aren't you?"

"But I . . . but I . . ." Sebastian watched miserably as the Princess swam off with the evil eels. He didn't want to go to her father, but he couldn't let Ariel go to the witch.

"Come on!" Sebastian called to Flounder.

He hopped onto Flounder's back. Flounder shot through the water to follow the Princess.

12

Flotsam and Jetsam led Ariel to a dark, eerie part of the ocean. They swam past a bed of strange, writhing plants that grabbed at Ariel and tried to pull her down.

"This way," hissed Flotsam and Jetsam. Ariel followed them into the witch's lair. Sebastian and Flounder trailed behind her and hid near the entrance.

The witch slid out of her shell. "Come in, my child," she said. "You're here because you have a thing for this human, this prince fellow, don't you? Well, angelfish, the solution to your problem is simple. The only way to get what you want is to become a human yourself."

"Can you do that?" Ariel gasped. She knew that the witch could make magic. But to turn a mermaid into a *human*. . . .

"My dear, sweet child," said Ursula. "I love to help unfortunate merfolk like yourself. Of course, when they fail to pay me for my services, I've sometimes been forced to turn the poor souls into little polyps and plant them in my garden."

"So that's what those strange plants were," Ariel shuddered.

The witch explained her plan. She would make a potion that would turn Ariel into a human for three days. But there was a catch. Ariel could remain human only if she could get the Prince to kiss her. And it had to be a kiss of true love. If the Prince did not kiss her by sunset on the third day, Ariel would turn back into a mermaid.

"And you'll belong to me!" Ursula cackled.

Sebastian poked his head out from his hiding place and called out to the Princess. "No, Ariel! Don't be stupid! Don't listen!"

"You could be the Prince's wife," Ursula sneered. "That's your dream, isn't it? Let me make it real.

"Oh, yes, I almost forgot," she added. "We haven't discussed the matter of payment."

"But I don't have anything to pay you with," said Ariel.

"I'm not asking much," said Ursula. "Just a token, really. A trifle. You'll never miss it. What I want from you is . . . your voice."

"My voice!" cried Ariel.

Ursula waved her hand, and a contract floated magically down before Ariel. Ariel was torn. If she signed, she would be signing away her voice

. . . and possibly her life! On the other hand, Ursula was offering her the chance to become human, the chance to win her beloved prince.

Ariel took the pen from Ursula's hand. She signed her name.

Ursula swam right to her cauldron. She said some magic words. The potion in the cauldron bubbled and steamed.

"Now, sing!" Ursula commanded.

Ariel opened her mouth and began to sing. Her sweet voice filled the cavernous room. Suddenly a pair of steamy hands rose out of the cauldron and grabbed Ariel by the throat. A soft, pink sphere came flying out of her open mouth. The hands caught the ball. It was Ariel's voice! Ursula grabbed the voice and held it in her greedy hands.

"Ha-ha!" she screeched.

Then with another wave of her hands, Ursula split Ariel's fin in two. Ariel struggled in the water. She could no longer swim! Her fins had become legs! She could no longer breathe! She had lungs, like a human! Flounder and Sebastian raced over and grabbed their friend under the arms. They whisked her up to the surface of the water. Ariel gasped for breath. The sea was no longer her home.

13

Back on land, Prince Eric was sitting outside his castle. He was gazing out to sea, thinking of the lovely girl who had saved his life. He reached over to pet Max, who was sitting right beside him.

"That voice!" he said sadly. "I can't get it out of my head. I've looked everywhere. Where could she be?"

The Prince did not know that the girl he was dreaming of was not very far from the castle. Sebastian and Flounder had dragged her to shore. Ariel was sitting at the edge of the water, kicking her new legs and wiggling her new toes.

As Sebastian walked on to the sand and Flounder splashed in the water, Scuttle flew down and landed beside Ariel.

"Well, look what the catfish dragged in," he said. "Look at you. There's something different." Scuttle cocked his head and squinted at his friend.

"Don't tell me. I've got it, it's your hairdo, right? No. Let me see, you got a tan?"

"She's got legs, you idiot!" shouted Sebastian. "Oh, what will her father say?" he wailed. "He's going to kill me! I've got to tell him."

Ariel could no longer speak, but she shook her head wildly. She lifted Sebastian up into her hand and gave him a kiss.

Sebastian sighed.

"All right," he said. "I'll try to help you find that prince."

Ariel grinned. She stood up on her wobbly legs and brushed the seaweed off of her.

"Now, Ariel," said Scuttle. "If you want to be a human, the first thing you've got to do is dress like one."

He grabbed a torn piece of sail that had washed up on the beach. He wrapped it around Ariel.

"You look great, kid!" He whistled.

Down the beach, Max jumped up from Eric's side. He sniffed the air. He took off, running down the shore.

"Max!" cried Eric. "What's gotten into you?"

Eric chased down the beach after his dog. Max stopped suddenly. He jumped up on his master. He licked Eric's face. Eric spotted the girl.

"Oh, I see," he said.

The girl was wet and bedraggled. She was clothed in tatters.

"Are you okay, miss?" Eric asked.

Ariel ducked her head in shame.

"I'm awfully sorry," Eric said, patting Max's head. "Did this knucklehead scare you?"

Ariel shook her head. Eric stared at her. She looked familiar to him somehow.

"Do I know you?" Eric asked. "Have we met?"

Ariel nodded her head and smiled.

"We have met! I knew it!" cried Eric. "You're the one I've been looking for! What's your name?"

For a moment, Ariel forgot that she had no voice. She opened her mouth to speak. Nothing came out.

"Oh," said Eric sadly. "You can't speak. Then you couldn't be who I thought you were."

Ariel waved her arms frantically and tried to speak again. She pointed to the sea. She had to make him understand!

"What is it?" asked Eric. "You're hurt? You need help?"

Ariel's legs wobbled underneath her.

"Careful," said Eric. "I'll help you."

He put his arm around her waist and led her down the shore. Sebastian jumped up and hid in a fold of Ariel's clothing.

"Come on," Eric said gently to Ariel. "I'll take you to the castle. You'll be okay."

14

Eric led Ariel through the tall entranceway and delivered her to Carlotta, who was the lady of the castle. Carlotta brought Ariel to a grand bathroom. She helped Ariel out of her wet clothes and filled a tub of warm water for the girl to bathe. She rang for a maid to launder Ariel's clothes. Poor Sebastian was still clinging to the fabric. He skittered onto the floor and into the halls of the great castle.

In the dining room, Prince Eric and Sir Grimsby were seated at the royal table, waiting for dinner. Eric was talking about the girl who had rescued him. He was still determined to find her.

"Oh, Eric," said Grimsby, "be reasonable. Nice young ladies just don't swim around rescuing people in the middle of the ocean and then flitter off into oblivion."

"I'm telling you, Grim," said Eric, "she was real! I'm going to find that girl and marry her!"

Carlotta led Ariel to the doorway of the dining

room. Ariel was now clean and was wearing a beautiful new dress. When she saw Eric, she hung back shyly.

"Come on, honey," Carlotta pulled her into the room.

Sir Grimsby was quite taken by the young girl's beauty. He rose from his seat to welcome her.

"Eric," he said. "Isn't she a vision? Come, come," he beckoned Ariel. "You must be famished."

Ariel took her place at the table. Before her was a very elegant place setting—beautiful china and a silver knife and fork. A dinglehopper! Ariel picked it up and ran it through her hair.

Sir Grimsby stared at the girl, perplexed. He took a puff on his pipe. Ariel recognized that, too. A snarfblatt! She took the pipe from Grimsby's hands and blew into it with all her breath. Ashes and soot came flying out of the bowl and splattered Grimsby's face.

Eric laughed out loud at the sight.

"Why, Eric," said Carlotta. "That's the first time I've seen you smile in weeks."

Grimsby wiped his face with his napkin.

"Carlotta, my dear," he said, trying to change the subject, "what's for dinner?"

"Oh, you're going to love it," Carlotta smiled. "It's the chef's specialty. Stuffed crab!"

* * *

In the kitchen, Louis the chef was preparing dinner. Sebastian wandered in.

"Zut alors!" said Louis, looking down. He thought he had missed one of the dinner crabs. Louis picked up Sebastian and dunked him in the special sauce. He sprinkled Sebastian with salt and pepper, and began stuffing onion into the little crab's shell. Just as he was about to toss Sebastian into a pot of boiling water, the crab pinched him on the nose. With an indignant shout, Louis dropped Sebastian, and Sebastian skittered away.

"So, Eric . . . " As they waited at the table, Sir Grimsby was trying to get Eric interested in Ariel. "Perhaps our young guest might enjoy seeing some sights of the kingdom, " he said with a wink. "Something in the way of a tour. You can't spend all your time moping about. You need to do something to get your mind off that girl."

Eric looked at Ariel. She did look beautiful. He liked her, too.

"Would you like to take a tour of the kingdom tomorrow?" he asked her.

Ariel nodded her head and smiled.

15

That night Eric was restless. As the others in the castle were getting ready for bed, Eric wandered outside with Max. He sat on a rock beneath Ariel's window. He glanced up at her lit pane.

"You like her, don't you, Max?" Eric asked his dog.

Max barked and nodded his shaggy head up and down. Eric put his arms around the dog.

"I like her, too," he said. He heaved a big sigh. "If only she were the girl!"

In her bedroom, Ariel was settling in under her covers. She'd never slept in a bed before. She burrowed her feet under the blanket and rested her head on the soft feather pillow.

Sebastian climbed up to the edge of her bed.

"We've got to make a plan to get that boy to kiss you," he said. "Tomorrow, when he takes you for that ride, you've got to bat your eyelashes. Like this," he said. He fluttered his own crusty eyelids. "And you've got to pucker up your lips. Like this." He pushed his lips out.

Sebastian scrambled across the pillow so Ariel could see, but Ariel's eyes were closed and her breathing soft and rhythmic. The girl was already asleep!

"You are hopeless, child, you know that?" Sebastian sighed. He pulled the covers up around her shoulders and tucked the Princess in.

That same night, back in the merworld, King Triton was in his throne room. He was worried about Ariel. He was swimming back and forth. A little seahorse messenger swam into his chambers.

"Any sign of them?" the King asked hopefully.

"No, Your Majesty," said the messenger. "We've found no trace of your daughter or Sebastian."

"Well, keep looking!" the King commanded. "Leave no shell unturned, no coral unexplored. Let no one in this kingdom sleep until she's safe at home!"

King Triton sank into his throne. He closed his eyes and buried his head in his hands.

"Oh, what have I done?" he cried. "What have I done?"

16

The next day, Eric took Ariel on a tour of the kingdom. They rode through the streets in the royal carriage. Ariel looked out the window, drinking in all the human sights. Sebastian hid in Ariel's pocket. He watched to see if Eric would kiss her. Eric did not.

Of the three days that Ariel had been granted, one had passed. Now there were only two left.

On the second day, Eric took Ariel for a boat ride around the lagoon. Eric sat at one end of the boat and rowed. Ariel sat at the other. Both looked shy and a little nervous. Scuttle flew watchfully overhead.

"Nothing is happening!" muttered Scuttle. "One day left and that boy ain't puckered up once."

Sebastian had an idea. He crawled over the side of the boat and into the water. He called together a group of colorful fish and luminescent sea creatures. They quickly assembled into a chorus. Sebastian raised his hands to conduct. The sea creatures began to sing.

"Kiss the girl," they sang. "Kiss the girl."

In the boat, Eric glanced up at the sound.

"Did you hear something?" he asked Ariel.

Ariel shrugged her shoulders and smiled.

The afternoon sun sparkled on Ariel's hair. Eric found himself wanting to kiss her, though he wasn't sure why.

Eric leaned closer to Ariel, but then he pulled back shyly.

"You know," he said, "I feel really bad not knowing your name. Well, maybe I could guess. Is it Kathryn?"

Ariel shook her head no.

"How about Diana?"

"Ariel!" Sebastian whispered from the water below. "Her name is Ariel!"

"Ariel," Eric said thoughtfully, as if he had thought of the name himself. "That's pretty."

"Kiss the girl," the chorus sang.

Eric smiled at the pretty princess. He leaned over and was about to kiss her, but as he did, his motion made the boat rock wildly. Eric lost his balance. The boat overturned. Ariel and Eric fell into the water!

From their vantage point under the boat, Flotsam and Jetsam sniggered slyly as they watched

Eric and Ariel struggle in the water.

"Hang on! I've got you!" Eric called. He grabbed Ariel by the waist and pulled her to shore.

Another day was gone. Eric had not kissed Ariel. Time was running out.

In her lair, Ursula had watched the whole scene in her pool of light.

"That was a close one," she sneered.

The witch swam to her cauldron and stirred the thick, steamy liquid inside.

"The girl's not going to get away from me that easily," she said. "This one's too important."

Ursula clutched the shell that hung around her neck. In the shell was Ariel's voice. Ursula stirred the witch's brew again. It began to bubble and churn. Ursula scooped up a handful of the potion and drank it greedily.

"Triton's daughter will be mine!" she cried.

As she drank the potion, she began to twitch and writhe. Her body was changing! Ursula was turning into a beautiful young woman!

Late that night, as the Prince sat looking moodily out to sea, he heard someone singing in the mist. He had heard that voice before! That song! It was the song of the girl who had saved him! Eric squinted out into the fog. A shadowy figure was walking toward him. It was a beautiful young maiden! She must be the girl!

17

The next morning, as the sun rose over the kingdom, Ariel lay snug and asleep in bed. Scuttle flew through her open bedroom window.

"Ariel! Wake up!" he cried. "I just heard the news. Congratulations, kiddo!"

Ariel opened her eyes and blinked sleepily.

"The Prince is getting married this afternoon!" Scuttle explained. "The whole town's buzzing!"

Ariel could hardly believe her ears. The Prince! Getting married! That must mean *she* was going to be his bride! Ariel threw on her robe and ran down the long palace stairway to find Eric. When she reached the bottom, though, she stopped short in surprise.

There in the hallway was Eric. With him was a young woman. Eric held her by the arm and stared straight ahead as the two talked to Sir Grimsby.

"Well, Eric," said Sir Grimsby, "so this mystery

maiden of yours does indeed exist. And she's lovely. Congratulations, my dear."

"Vanessa and I are going to be married this afternoon," said Eric, as if in a daze. "The wedding ship will depart at sunset."

Ariel's eyes welled up with tears. Eric was going to marry someone else! Ariel ran crying from the room as Grimsby congratulated the happy couple.

By late that afternoon, preparations for the wedding were almost completed. The wedding ship was decorated with banners and bows. Eric was on deck, waiting for his bride. The ship set sail.

Ariel sat forlornly on the pier. She slumped against a post and cried. She watched the boat as it sailed out toward the horizon.

Scuttle still thought the wedding was to be Ariel's. He flew down to the boat to wish the Princess luck. There, in a chamber below deck, he stumbled upon Vanessa. She was powdering her face and adjusting her wedding gown. This bride wasn't Ariel! Scuttle stared at her in horror.

The young maiden adjusted an odd shell that hung around her neck, then admired herself in the mirror. Scuttle looked at her reflection. It wasn't a young woman at all! The face in the mirror was Ursula's!

"The sea witch!" cried Scuttle. "Oh, no! She's going to marry the Prince! Somebody's got to stop her!"

Scuttle flew quickly back to shore and found Ariel on the pier. Sebastian and Flounder were there, too, trying their best to comfort her.

"The Prince is marrying the sea witch in disguise!" cried Scuttle.

Ariel gasped. She dove into the water to swim to the boat. Sebastian rolled a barrel into the water to buoy her. He had a plan.

"Ariel, grab onto that," he called. "Flounder, you pull her to the boat as fast as your fins can carry you. I've got to get to the Sea King! He must know about this!"

"What about me?" asked Scuttle.

"You find a way to stall the wedding," Sebastian instructed.

"Stall the wedding?" moaned Scuttle. "That would take an army." The gull scratched his head. "An army! That's it!" he cried.

Scuttle took off into the air, loudly squawking the alarm. Birds listened from their trees. Seals stirred on their rocks. Scuttle needed help! It was an emergency! The animals flocked to Scuttle, responding to his call. Scuttle had recruited an army!

18

As Flounder pulled Ariel out to the ship, Eric and the evil Vanessa took their places before the minister.

"Dearly beloved," the minister began the ceremony.

"Don't worry, Ariel," Flounder assured his friend. "We're going to make it."

On the ship, Vanessa looked slyly up at Eric. The minister continued.

"Do you, Eric," he asked, "take Vanessa to be your lawfully wedded wife for as long as you both shall live?"

"I do," said Eric, still in a strange daze.

The minister smiled. He started to pronounce the two husband and wife. But before he could finish his sentence, a loud cawing sound interrupted the ceremony. It was Scuttle! And behind him were hundreds of other birds! Vanessa looked up in alarm. The birds swooped down to attack her. They dove at her head. They pecked at her arms.

"Get away from me," Vanessa screeched. "You slimy little — "

Eric looked at his bride in surprise. Vanessa was not the sweet-voiced young maiden he had thought.

"Oh, Eric," Vanessa said quickly, trying again to disguise her voice. "I'm so frightened!"

The birds dove down at her. Vanessa screeched again.

Just then, Ariel and Flounder reached the side of the ship. Ariel hoisted herself up on the oars and climbed over the railing.

"Ariel?" Eric said, surprised.

Eric looked at Ariel. She was wet and bedraggled. He looked at Vanessa, who was angrily fighting off Scuttle. Scuttle was tugging at the shell that hung from Vanessa's neck. He yanked the shell free. It fell to the ground and shattered. Ariel's voice bounced out and flew back up to her throat.

"Eric," Ariel said weakly.

"Ariel! You can talk!" cried Eric. "You're the one!"

He rushed to Ariel's side.

"Eric!" screamed Vanessa. "Get away from her!"

Eric ignored the witch. He took Ariel's hands in his.

"It was you all the time," he said.

"Oh, Eric," cried Ariel. "I wanted to tell you."

Eric took Ariel in his arms and leaned closer to kiss her. But just as their lips were about to meet, Vanessa began to cackle hideously. As the crowd watched in horror, Vanessa changed from a young maiden back into the evil sea witch, Ursula.

Ursula flung her arms around angrily. Ariel's legs wobbled and she collapsed onto the deck. She looked down. Her legs were gone. She had a tail again! Ursula had turned Ariel back into a mermaid!

Eric looked down at Ariel's tail in shock. Ursula grabbed the mermaid and clutched her tightly.

"You're too late!" she cackled. She threw herself overboard, taking Ariel with her. "So long, loverboy!"

Ursula dove down to her lair, dragging Ariel with her.

Eric quickly climbed into a lifeboat and lowered it down into the water.

"Eric! What are you doing?" cried Sir Grimsby.

"I lost her once," Eric called back. "I'm not going to lose her again!"

19

Ursula plunged through the water with her captive.

"Poor little princess," she leered. "It's not you I'm after. I've a much bigger fish to fry."

Suddenly in front of her the water sparked and crackled. There was King Triton. His spear was aimed at Ursula.

"Let my daughter go!" he commanded.

"Not a chance, Triton," Ursula laughed. "She's mine. We made a deal."

Ursula waved her arm. The contract that Ariel had signed floated down in front of the king. Ursula waved her arms again. She turned Ariel into one of her wriggling, snakelike plants.

"Ha-ha!" Ursula laughed. "You see? The contract's legal and binding!"

King Triton looked in horror at his poor daughter. She was struggling to get free. Ursula dangled the contract before the King.

"Now," Ursula said slyly, "do we have a deal?"

She knew that Triton would sacrifice himself to save his daughter.

King Triton lowered his head in defeat. He reached for the contract. His name magically appeared in place of Ariel's. Ariel changed back into a mermaid, but the King himself began to shrivel. He was becoming a captive plant in Ursula's evil garden!

King Triton's crown and spear fell to the ocean floor. Ursula grabbed for them. She lifted the crown to her own head and raised the spear high in the waters.

"At last!" she cried. "Now *I* am ruler of all the ocean!"

Suddenly a harpoon shot through the water and struck the witch in the shoulder.

It was Eric! He had come to save Ariel!

"Eric!" Ariel called to him. "You have to get away from here!"

Eric rushed to the surface for air. Ariel streaked through the water after him. The two lovers reached each other and embraced. But they were not safe yet. Eight long tentacles rose out of the water, surrounding them on all sides. It was Ursula. She had them trapped. Ariel and Eric huddled together in fear.

"You pitiful, insignificant fools," Ursula hissed. "I am now Queen of the Ocean! The waves obey my every whim."

Then Ursula began to get bigger. Up she rose out of the sea. With her trident she created a huge wave. It separated Eric from Ariel and cast the Prince into the churning waters. The Prince struggled against the waves and swam to his ship.

Ursula looked down at Ariel. She raised her spear and aimed it at the Princess.

"Eric!" screamed Ariel.

Just as Ursula was about to drive the spear into Ariel's heart, Eric reached the ship's helm. He grabbed the wheel and spun it around. He aimed the ship right at Ursula. The ship shot through the waves and gored the witch.

"Agggh!" Ursula screamed. The water bubbled up, steamimg and hissing. Soon nothing was left but a slick of black ooze. Eric swam wearily to shore.

At the bottom of the sea, as the witch died, a light encircled King Triton and all the other souls who had been prisoners in the witch's garden. The prisoners were freed!

The evil witch was dead. Her wicked spells no longer held any power.

20

As the seas calmed, Ariel pulled herself up on a rock and saw Eric lying unconscious in the distance.

King Triton rose to the surface of the water and watched his daughter from afar. He turned to Sebastian beside him.

"She really does love him, doesn't she?" the King said softly.

Sebastian nodded his head.

"Children have to be free to live their own lives," Sebastian said.

King Triton sighed. He knew what he must do.

"Then I guess there's just one problem left," he said.

"What's that, Your Majesty?" asked Sebastian.

"How much I'm going to miss her," the King said sadly.

King Triton pointed his magic spear into the water. Its current traveled on the waves to the rock where Ariel sat. Suddenly Ariel was surrounded by a beautiful light. She looked down. Her tail was washing away, and in its place were two human legs!

Eric opened his eyes. He saw the Princess walking toward him out of the water. The two fell into each other's arms. Finally they kissed, with the soft ocean mist spraying up around them.

That very day, the two were married. Ariel took her rightful place at the Prince's side on board the wedding ship. Beside the ship, all the merpeople gathered in the water to wish Ariel well. The minister pronounced the two husband and wife, and everyone cheered.

Ariel plucked a rose from her bouquet and tossed it over the side of the boat to her father. As the wedding ship sailed off into the mist, Ariel waved good-bye. Eric joined his bride and put his arm around her waist.

Ariel had found her dream. She was married to her prince. And the little mermaid was human at last.

You'll love

Walt Disney's ®

CLASSICS

Remember how much you loved Walt Disney movies? Now's your chance to read all the Disney Classics! You'll love these fantastic stories…starring your favorite Disney characters and illustrated with photos taken directly from the movie!

Read them all!

- ☐ 41170-5 **Snow White and the Seven Dwarfs**
- ☐ 41450-X **Lady and the Tramp**
- ☐ 41171-3 **Cinderella**
- ☐ 41172-1 **The Fox and the Hound**
- ☐ 41664-2 **Bambi**
- ☐ 42049-6 **Oliver & Company**

Prefix code 0-590-

Available wherever you buy books…or use the coupon below.
$2.50 each.

© 1988 The Walt Disney Company